For Neal

WALTER WAS WORRIED

Laura Vaccaro Seeger

SQUARE
FISH

ROARING BROOK PRESS

NEW YORK

Walter was

worried

when

the sky grew

dark.

Priscilla was

PUZZLEd

when

the fog rolled

in.

Shirley was

SHOCKED

when

lightning lit the

sky.

Frederick was

FRIGHTENED

when

thunder shook the

trees.

Ursula was

upset

when

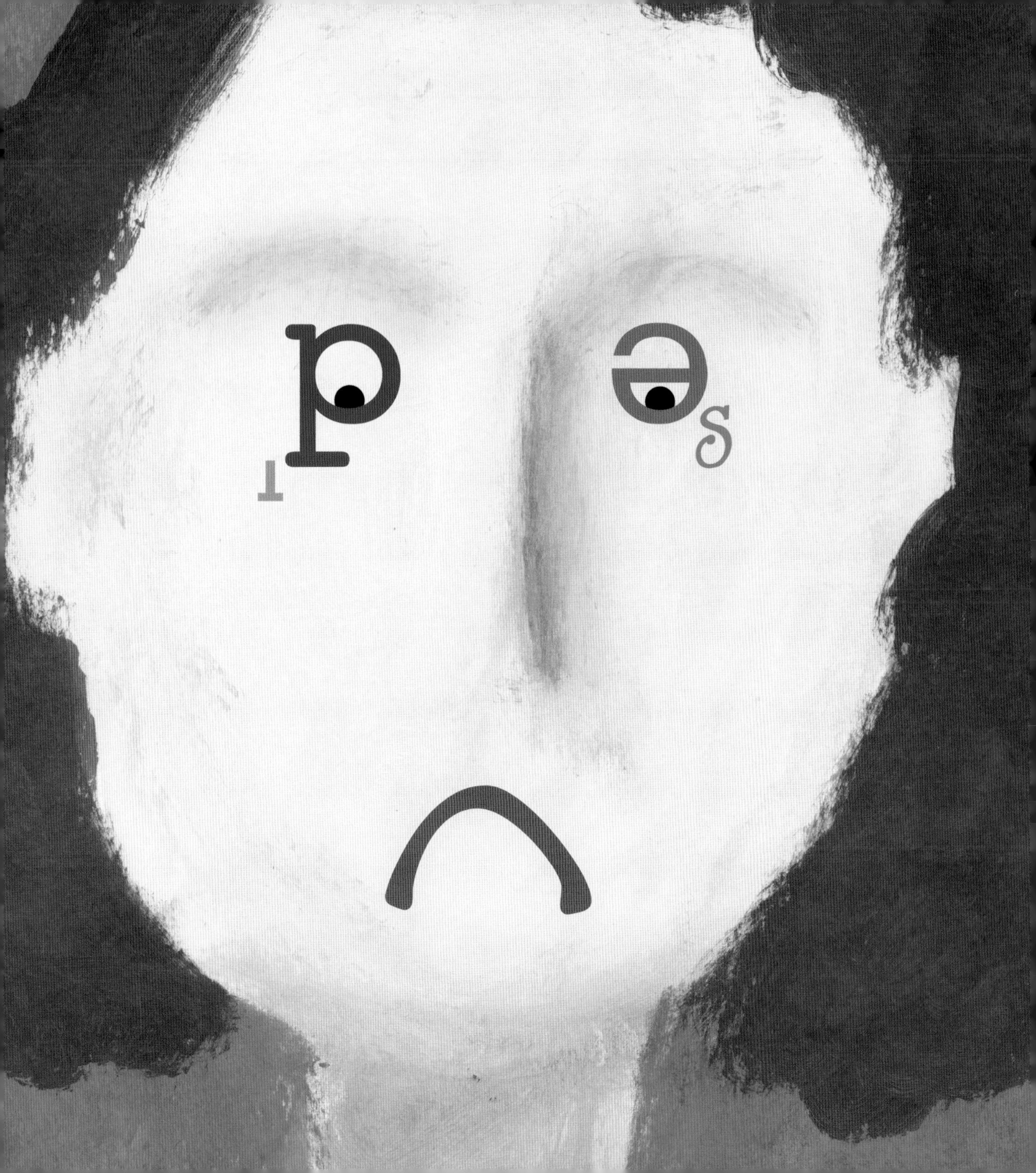

the rain came

down.

Then...

Delilah was

DELIGHTED

when

the rain turned to

snow.

Henry was

HOPEFUL

when

the sky began to

clear.

And...

Elliot was

ECSTATIC

when

the sun came

out.

SQUARE
FISH
An Imprint of Macmillan

Library of Congress Cataloging-in-Publication Data
Seeger, Laura Vaccaro.
Walter was worried / Laura Vaccaro Seeger.
p.   cm.
"A Neal Porter book."
Summary: Children's faces, depicted with letters of the alphabet,
react to the onset of a storm and its aftermath in this picture book,
accompanied by simple alliterative text.
ISBN 978-1-59643-196-6
[1. Storms—Fiction. 2. Emotions—Fiction. 3. Alliteration.] I. Title.
PZ7.S4514Wal 2005   [E]—dc22   2004024558

Originally published in the United States by Roaring Brook Press
First Square Fish Edition: August 2012
Square Fish logo designed by Filomena Tuosto
mackids.com

20 19 18 17 16 15 14 13

WALTER WAS WORRIED

"A wonderful collaboration of art and story."
—*School Library Journal*

"Moods can change as quickly as the weather, and this innovative concept book cleverly illustrates the range and volatility of both."
—*Kirkus Reviews*

An ALA Notable Book
A *Child* Magazine Best Book of the Year

Other Inventive Concept Books by LAURA VACCARO SEEGER

THE HIDDEN ALPHABET

An ALA Notable

A *Child* Magazine
Best Book of the Year

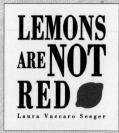

LEMONS ARE NOT RED

An ALA Notable

A *Child* Magazine
Best Book of the Year

BLACK? WHITE! DAY? NIGHT!

Discover an extravaganza of opposites in this imaginative book